Nonna's Little Meatballs

make pasta

Written and Illustrated by J. Falcone

This book is dedicated to Reid, Adrianna, Olivia, Willow, Charlotte, Rose, Josephine and the two new babies on the way.

my husband Dale,
our children,
my mom,
and my grandmother
who gave me lasting, loving memories in her kitchen, making pasta.

I love you all so much

Nonna's "little meatballs"
make something good to eat!

Sometimes it's something salty,
sometimes it's something sweet...

but Nonna always makes for us,
what we are dreaming of.

It's made with something special…
it's always made with love.

We love to cook with Nonna

because it's so much fun!

Today we're making pasta

until the day is done.

She puts flour on the table,
and then she makes a well.

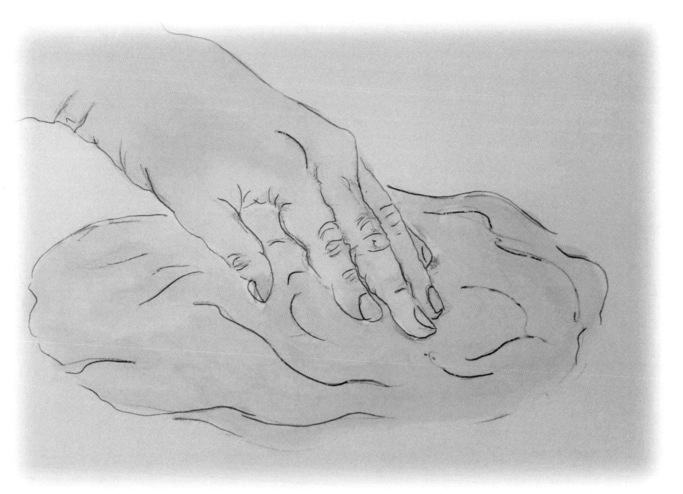

She puts in eggs and scrambles…
It's like a magic spell!

The eggs and flour mix together,
there's flour everywhere!

It's sticky and it's messy,
but Nonna doesn't care!

Everyone waits their turn
to use the pasta machine.

To make enough for dinner
We have to be a team!

We put it through the top,
and turn the handle for a while.

We flatten it and flatten it,

until Nonna has a smile.

When it's really, really flat
it's ready to push on through,

the cutter that will make spaghetti,
for Nonna, her "meatballs", and you.

The noodles come out skinny

and turn into little strings,

then we dry them on a rack…

they look like pasta swings!

When the pasta strings are dry,
Nonna puts them in a pot.

They cook until they float,
but watch out! They're very hot!

Nonna drains the water out,

then adds sauce and
cheese.

Everyone giggles when Jo Jo says,

"Nonna, sketti please!"

We smile, eat and laugh,
and have a little bread.

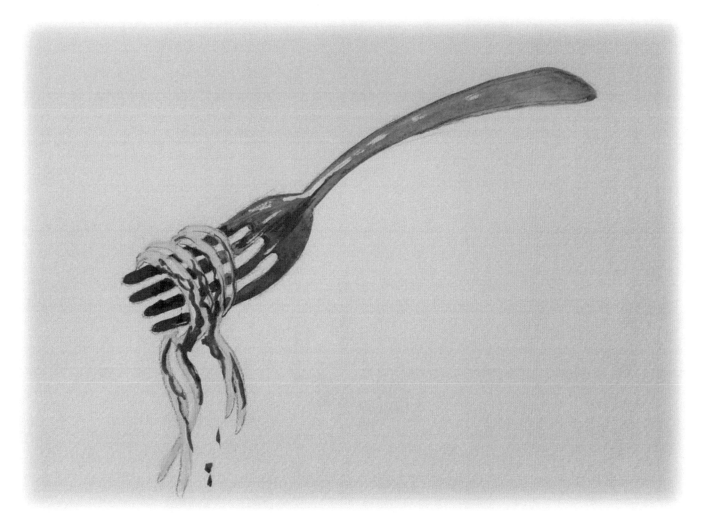

We roll it on our forks…
until our tummy's spread.

When we are done, we get a kiss,

and then we go and play,

until Nonna's
"little meatballs"

cook
another
day.

The End

Now for the recipe:

Homemade Pasta

Ingredients: (makes 3 servings about 175 calories)

1 cup all-purpose flour   2 large eggs   1 Tbsp Salt for the water

1. Put ¾ cup of the flour on the table into a mound and make a well in the middle.
2. Crack an egg into the well. (you may want to crack it in a bowl first so you can take out any unwanted shells)
3. With a fork, scramble the eggs in the well.
4. Then with your hands, draw the flour into the eggs until it comes together. Once the eggs are incorporated into the flour, knead it with your hands a little…about 3-4 minutes; (if it's too sticky, slowly add remaining flour and more if need be, but don't make it dry). It should feel like play dough.
5. Cover it with plastic wrap and let it rest about a half hour.
6. After it rests, take it out of the plastic and cut it in half. Roll it out with a rolling pin or pasta machine. Use more flour to keep it from sticking while rolling.
7. When it is flat enough, cut it into strips using a knife or pasta machine.
8. You can cook it right away or dry it on a rack to eat later.

To cook it:
1. Boil water in a large pot. Enough that the pasta is not crowded.
2. Add the salt to the water.
3. Add your pasta.
4. Let it cook until it starts to float to the top. (about 4-5 minutes)
5. Drain the water out using a colander.
6. Add sauce and eat!

Special thank you to

cait rose Photography

for the following beautiful and memorable pictures.

Made in the USA
Las Vegas, NV
23 March 2024

87587419R00017